Yuletide Tales

Short Story Collection

Power Places Series

Theresa Crater

Crystal Star
PUBLISHING

Crystal Star Publishing
1303 Alexandria St.
Lafayette, CO 80026
www.theresacraterbooks.com

Yuletide Tales
By Theresa Crater

Cover image by Willgard on Pixabay

Printed in the United States of America
Worldwide Electronic & Digital Rights
1 st North American and UK Print Rights

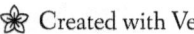 Created with Vellum

For Austin

Frankincense and Myrrh

What a nice Jewish boy was doing lying under a Christmas tree carefully studying the ornaments, Michael couldn't easily explain. Partly he was blocking Arthur from pulling off the decorations. The boy had grown into a strapping ten-month old, crawling at lightning speed and grabbing hold of anything to pull himself up to his feet.

And then there were the Egyptian Maus. Merlin climbed. The lower limbs supported him, but the cat insisted on going for the top, threatening to topple the whole tree more than once. Vivienne was fascinated by her reflection in the colored glass ornaments. At first, she'd poke them gently, but soon one would get knocked off and the two would swat it around. They'd broken four family heirlooms already. Anne worried about them cutting their paws, but Grandmother Elizabeth cared more about her decorations. She proposed banning them from the large formal living room the tree occupied, but there were just too many ways to get into the room. Especially for cats.

But Michael was an archaeologist. That was the real reason he was gazing up into the boughs of the Douglas fir.

"There's an ancient artifact hidden among the Christmas decorations," Anne had said. "Go find it. But let it speak to you," she pointed to the middle of her forehead, "in your mind."

He was cheating, of course, running through the list of what a relic would look like, where the Le Clairs might have come across it—Egypt, France, England. Even Atlantis, if he was to believe Grandmother Elizabeth. And he did.

It had all started a few days ago when Michael confessed to harboring some jealousy over Anne's psychic abilities. "I mean, you just took to it like—" he searched for a fresh metaphor in vain "—a duck to water."

"But Dr. Abernathy did train me," she objected.

"For a month, maybe. Most people have to work years to unfold a tenth of what you can do."

"Yeah, but you know like—everything."

Michael laughed. "That's quite the exaggeration."

"Seriously. At every site in Egypt, you could go on for hours at a time and still tell me something new at dinner. Then you knew all about Glastonbury."

"I'm an anthropologist. And an Egyptologist."

"Khemitologist," she automatically corrected him. Tahir preferred to use the name of the ancient civilization. "Plus, you know more myth than a classics professor."

"Still, I'd love to be able to see what you see. To feel what people are feeling."

"No, you wouldn't," Anne said. "It's downright aggravating to know what people really feel while they're lying to your face."

Michael chuckled. "There is that."

"Besides, you saw lots of things in Egypt and in England."

"I've opened my senses some, but remember I've been training for years. You're a bit of a savant."

"Michael," she whispered, pulling him closer, her skin warm against his chest.

He leaned in to kiss her, but before the kiss deepened, a small projectile landed on top of him, squirming and wriggling, then inserting itself between them. Arthur crowed his pleasure, then proceeded to chatter, inserting the few words he knew into his stream of contented nonsense.

Michael stroked his son's head. "Where did all this blond hair come from?"

"Me, I guess," Anne said. "But he has your mouth."

Michael tilted the child's face toward his to study it for the millionth time.

"Da," Arthur said and grabbed Michael's chin.

"Think he'll be as psychic as you are?"

"Oh, stop." Anne sat up and took the child in her arms, letting him nurse. "I know what you need."

"What's that?" Michael leaned back, admiring his very own Madonna and child.

"A treasure hunt." And that's when she'd challenged him to find the artifact.

Now under the tall fir, Michael let his eyes roam up through the branches crowded with colored balls, stars, small figurines, and symbols from all the religions of the world.

Footsteps approached. "Time for a bath, young man." Arthur's nanny claimed the child and carried him off to the nursery, leaving Michael with just the cats to worry about.

The string of faery lights—that's how he thought of them— lit the ornaments, subtly changing the colors, and illuminated the clear globes. Really, a nice Christmas tree was a wonder. He was glad he felt at home in all the traditions. Hanukah had come early this year and they'd spent it with his family in the city.

Something glinted at him from a branch about halfway up the tree. He slid out from beneath the large, lower boughs and stood, reorienting himself. Where had it been?

Michael pushed aside a smiling Santa and lifted the branch he hung on ever so gently. He was rewarded with the sight of a small wicker nest topped by a cardinal, too red to be a female, but he dismissed that objection. The bird sat on a treasure trove of little gemstones—rose quartz, topaz, lapis, moonstones, and clear quartz. Or was that one a diamond? Surely not.

Carefully he lifted each stone out, held it in the palm of his hand, closed his eyes, and waited to see what images would arise. The rose sent him a wave of gentle love, the lapis an image of Isis—but it was just a picture, not a living consciousness to interact with. None of the stones seemed to be the artifact.

He stepped back, almost tripping over a big box that had once held a set of weights Arnold had asked for. The debris of Christmas morning littered the floor—red, green, and gold wrapping paper, discarded boxes once containing surprises. Arnold had ignored the instructions of Grandmother Elizabeth to be careful and not tear the textured paper. No hope for the bows, either. Ribbon lay in streams on the floor and draped over the nearby couch and chairs.

Michael gathered an armful to carry to a box now serving as a collection bin. Merlin gave chase to the trailing ends, pulling half the load from Michael's arms. He tossed the remaining ribbon into the container and turned back to study the tree. He held both hands out, using them like antenna, feeling for any strong energy emanating from the Douglas fir. Nothing caught his attention.

Except a loud thud from behind him. The box now lay on

its side, paper and ribbon erupting from it. Merlin came flying out, a piece of blue tinsel in his mouth.

"No, you can't eat that." Michael gave chase and caught the cat halfway into the dining room where Estelle was supervising putting the final touches on the gleaming mahogany table.

"Scat," she cried, leaning over and clapping her hands at the cat.

Michael grabbed the tinsel as Merlin streaked by and it came loose easily. Merlin stopped and waited for him to dangle it.

"Why don't you show me where it is?" he asked him. "You've got the right name."

"Have you lost something?" Estelle asked.

"Oh, no. Anne has me on a treasure hunt."

"I see." She didn't, nor did she care to. She was too busy preparing the magical feast that would crown the evening. Estelle turned back to the table where Mr. Bowers, the butler, had taken out a measuring stick and moved a salad fork millimeters to the left.

Michael crept out of the room, a bit out of his depth. For him, Christmas Day had usually been Chinese take-out, then a movie, unless he spent it with Robert's family. The memory of his old mentor at the head of the table cutting the turkey, laughing with his grandchildren, made Michael pause in the hallway. He missed his steady hand and wise counsel. Perhaps he and Anne could take Arthur over for an evening with Robert's remaining family before the holidays ended and everyone scattered to jobs and universities.

Michael still served as head of the group Robert had led and passed on to him at his death, Lodge Rose Croix, where Michael had done his metaphysical studies and initiations. This year at the winter solstice, his group had been invited to a grand ritual combining Grandmother Elizabeth's Lodge of Isis and the most elite group in the Americas, Valentin Knight's Lodge of Melchizedek. Knight had been instrumental in clearing the way for Arthur's birth and since then, the family had grown closer to him. The ceremony had been quite an honor, not to mention a deep spiritual experience. Given how open Michael had been that night, he should be able to solve Anne's little puzzle. He turned his attention to the task at hand.

He walked through the large house, letting himself drift into a light trance. Three white ceramic angels stood in a niche near Grandmother Elizabeth's office, tall and ethereal, holding golden globes that glowed at night. Elizabeth had lectured Arthur on the dangers of the angel hair surrounding their bases, and he had made a grab for some as soon as she was done. Arthur's great grandmother persisted in talking to him as if he were at least eight. Michael paused before the statues and considered the energy. Nothing pulled at him.

He meandered back to the front of the house and paused before the mantel above the fireplace in the sitting room. It looked like another formal living room to him, but less cavernous and with cozier chairs. The old brick of the fireplace had been softened with a wash of white and above a long mantel of rustic chapel white sported big swaths of evergreen tied up with bright red ribbons. Tiny stars dotted the boughs.

Family pictures filled the space, rather formal portraits before the giant tree in the living room, the people growing up and maturing in the images, some disappearing. Michael paused before a picture of President Le Clair sitting on a sofa holding an infant and completely overtaken by children, some teens, other younger, one making faces at the camera. Clusters of figurines sat interspersed between the pictures. He picked up one of the elves and turned it over. 'Made in Germany' it read in blue letters. Maybe over a hundred years old, but no artifact. Next came Santa on his sleigh, the reindeer soft to the touch. One naturally sported a red nose. Then a small creche. Next a little drummer boy painted in shining reds and blues, his drum trimmed in gold. Red candles surrounded by holly waited to be lit for the evening.

Maybe the artifact was outside. Michael went out the French doors leading to one of the side gardens and walked out on the green lawn, then turned to survey the house. Electric candles stood from each window, waiting to be switched on. The star-shaped reflecting pool had been drained for the winter, but a new star hung from the domed portico—Michael couldn't call such a grand structure a porch. It had been a gift from Valentin Knight, a Moravian star, something special from an adventure he had been a part of a few years back. The symmetrical polyhedral sported sixty-four points and was truly a marvel.

But this was a new addition. Not the artifact he was seeking. Blast if he was going to let Anne best him. Not after he'd actually walked through time last February to help their child be born. He had to admit, though, he'd had a lot of assistance then.

Dusk approached and someone began turning on the candles in the windows. Soon the house glowed in the growing dark. Then the big star gleamed out, filling his heart with a matching golden glow. He walked under it through the front door into the grand entry hall, his shoes squeaking on the Italian tiled floor.

Someone was softly humming a Christmas carol. It sounded like "We Three Kings." He looked up and saw Anne leaning over the banister.

"Hurry up. We dress for Christmas dinner," she said.

"You aren't going to win, you know."

"Looks like I might."

"Another half hour."

"All right, but I'll need help with Arthur." She walked back down the hall toward their suite of rooms, humming again.

Then he remembered Grandmother Elizabeth had insisted the doors to the ballroom stay closed against "the mischief makers." She'd meant his son and Anne's cats. Michael trotted through the living room where two helpers hired for the holidays were cleaning up. He pulled the door open and slipped inside.

The room was dark, filled with the hushed quiet of a sanctuary. A familiar scent, deep and aromatic, reached him, but try as he might, he couldn't place it. He toed off his shoes. Reached for the light but stopped. The harsh overhead would not do.

He remembered two truncated columns supporting enormous pillar candles stood on either side the display to his right. The candles in the windows gave off just enough light for him to find the long-stemmed matches next to one of the tall cabinets. With a flick, he lit the candles, careful of the large bouquets of red roses in front of each column. He stood back and took it all in.

A large creche filled the width of the far wall. A wooden manger stuffed with straw sheltered two almost life-size figures, one standing, arms outstretched in protection. Joseph wore a maroon robe and dark golden sash. Mary leaned over a cradle, her robe the traditional blue of the Madonna, with a white headcover. Golden halos shown above both their heads. Two shepherds stood to one side, their faces a picture of awe and reverence. A lamb wandered close to the cradle. In the back, a donkey stretched out its nose. A cow stood beside it, its horns rounded, looking suspiciously like Hathor. Doves nestled in the overhanging wood beam, gazing down adoringly.

Above them all hovered angels adorned in white robes with golden wings spread. But the Le Clairs had not settled for just any angels. Here stood the four archangels—Michael with his golden sword, Gabriel with his trumpet just pulled away from his lips, Uriel carrying a round disk with the word *Sol,* and primary among them, glorious Raphael with a censor.

The three kings approached the Christ child who lay in the manger. Michael knew this manger represented earth, or the lowest sphere on the Tree of Life, the World where all became manifest. The divine consciousness born on earth. It was said the Divine One incarnated at the beginning of each major cycle to lead the world to the light. Christians, of course, believed this to be the one and only. Either way, the world celebrated the return of good at this time of year. The child lay, sweet and pure, swaddled in white cloth, the halo brighter than any others.

His teachers approached, the wise kings, bringing gifts. One figure dressed in rich purple held gold coins, the strength of the solar light. The second, his robes scarlet trimmed in pure white, held a small crock filled with golden chunks of resin.

Frankincense. Yes, it was a tree resin.

Michael crept closer and took a deep whiff. The scent of pine mixed with lemon reached his nose, followed close by a dry woody aroma.

The third figure wore royal blue and carried what looked like a small stone cup. Myrrh, Michael thought, the scent of Isis. A gift from the mother to the mother. And with a start, he realized this third king had a distinctly feminine face.

He laughed. Leave it to the Le Clairs.

On tiptoe, he waved his hand over the cup, bringing the scent to his nose. A nutty sweetness filled his senses. Definitely myrrh.

But wait.

Michael looked back at the small chalice in the hands of the third mage and studied it more closely. What he had taken as the yellow tone of the myrrh oil was really the vessel itself. He was looking at an alabaster cup. Could it be?

The woman with the alabaster jar was the phrase that had passed down in history. Mary Magdalene washed the feet of her Beloved and then anointed them with oil of spikenard.

But was this the actual vessel she had used? Had it survived in the possession of this special family?

Michael closed his eyes and asked for guidance. He waited in the reverent silence. After a few minutes, a beam of light touched his forehead and inside he saw a face. Dressed in blue with a white scarf over her head, she smiled at him, her expression joyous, radiant.

"Yes, beloved of my daughter, you have found me."

Mary Magdalene. The favorite disciple. The beloved of Yeshua.

She came close and kissed him on the top of his head and for a moment he was lost to the radiance that sparked up from that kiss.

When he came to, he heard something shift behind him. He turned to find Anne and Grandmother Elizabeth smiling from the doorway.

"Blessings to you, my grandson." Elizabeth made a sign with her hands.

Anne smiled. "I see you finally found it."

Festival of Lights

Anne took Michael's arm as they exited the subway. "I'm glad the dates worked out this year."

"Me, too."

"Grandmother Elizabeth thought it was important we both participate in the winter solstice ritual, after all that happened."

"I'm glad we could do it.

"You survived the grand soiree."

"I've never seen so many dignitaries."

"Thanks for taking care of my mother once she had too much to drink."

"I actually like your mother."

She squeezed his arm. "Miracles never cease."

"Mommy, mommy!" Arthur stopped in the middle of the sidewalk and pointed at the golden angels standing in front of the Christmas tree in Rockefeller Plaza.

Anne guided the toddler out of the way of the press of people and crouched down beside him. "Angels. They're holding horns."

Arthur's eyes were big, amazed by the sight.

"Aren't they beautiful?"

The child nodded, mesmerized.

"Wait until they light the tree," Michael said. "We'll see it on our way home."

He took Arthur's hand and led him back to the mass of humanity making their way down the sidewalk. "The family is looking forward to seeing us."

"So everyone gathers the first night of Chanukah?"

"Yes, it's not a big holiday, but it is a good time to get together, so it's become a tradition."

"Then Christmas Eve candlelight service tomorrow. Another festival of lights."

"I suppose so. I'm getting exhausted," Michael said.

"Me, too. We can rest in January."

"You haven't seen Uncle Ezra's apartment above the shop yet, have you?"

"No."

"He has the whole top floor."

"In the Diamond District? I thought you came from modest means," Anne teased.

"Did I say Uncle Ezra was sharing?"

She laughed. "He'd help out, I'm sure."

Michael changed the subject. "How did you first find his shop, anyway?"

"Somebody at the law firm recommended it. Your uncle has quite the reputation, apparently."

"I'm glad I was there that day."

"Yes, how could you not have been?" She took Arthur's other hand and the three made their way through the crowds of tourists and newscasters.

"Here's the shop," Michael said. He pushed open the door and the same bell that Anne remembered tinkled. But instead a rush of warm air smelling faintly of dust and cinnamon, the scent of desert sand under a hot sun filled the air.

She ran smack into Michael, who had stopped dead just inside the shop. Or what should be the shop.

Before them stood the golden stone walls of Jerusalem. But instead of just the wailing wall, the completed temple rose triumphant on the level above. Its gold doors and column tops glinted in the sun. The pink marble columns glowed.

"What happened?" Michael asked.

A war cry rang out in Hebrew, but somehow it translated in Anne's head. "I am Judah the Maccabee, and I declare the temple restored to us, Antiochus."

But the battle wasn't over yet. Men grappled with each other. The air filled with the ring of swords meeting, the shouts and grunts of soldiers in combat, the coppery scent of blood.

The ghostly shadow of a counter displaying antique necklaces stretched to the right. Michael grabbled Arthur up in one arm and ran for it, pulling Anne behind him.

The battle raged in front of them.

"What is it with this kid?" Michael asked.

"What are you talking about?"

"This is just like the battle I was in before Arthur was born."

"But this isn't Wales. Who are these people?"

"He said he was a Maccabee. Judah and his four brothers led the battle for the second temple of Jerusalem."

"How is this possible? Anne asked.

"Ask your son," Michael said.

"Oh, he's my son now."

Michael pushed a dark lock of hair out of his eyes. "We both travelled through time while you were in labor. This is the event Chanukah is based on."

Sudden silence fell and the scene morphed. Standing the

wall again, Judah shook his sword at a cloud of dust in the distance.

Anne could just make out the rumps of horses and foot soldiers struggling in the sand, an army escaping. Around them lay the bodies of men from both armies, bloodied, arms hacked away, mouths open in the pain of death.

Anne grabbed Arthur's arm and pushed him behind her.

"Mommy," he protested.

"I don't want him to see this," Anne said to Michael.

The bodies dissolved.

"What the—" Michael's mouth hung open.

"Uh, thank you?" Anne said tentatively.

The three of them hunched behind the counter. Incongruously, Anne stared at a ghostly diamond necklace laid out on black velvet, its three tiers sparkling under the sunlight. She looked up and watched the survivors gather in front of the wall. A battered wooden door opened and the man who'd been on top of the wall came through. "Let us remove the idols of the Seleucids." He gestured for everyone to follow.

"Who?" Anne asked.

"The Syrian-Greek Empire ruled Israel around 170-something BCE."

Anne made a choking sound.

"Don't worry." Michael knocked on the glass of the case they huddled behind. It sounded solid enough. "I think we're still in 2019."

The men crowded into the temple and on the second level they could see them milling around in the outer courtyard. They began picking up statues in teams and carrying them to the edge of the wall. With shouts of triumph, they tossed the marble sculptures over. Anne watched as figurines of Zeus and Hera broke into several pieces on the ground around the temple wall. Next came Artemis, then her brother, Apollo, behind her. The helmeted head of Athena rolled close. Anne stared into the goddess's serene marble eyes.

Soon the statues stopped falling. Three priests in white robes opened the doors to the Holy of Holies, gesturing for the men to enter. The army hesitated, but the priests encouraged them to come forward.

"We must cleanse the temple. Sweep the floors, then wash them. Remove the rest of the idols."

The afternoon wore on, but Anne didn't feel the passage of time. It was as if they were watching a movie, the main events presented to them in little vignettes. That afternoon or perhaps several days later, when the sun was halfway down the western sky, the men filed out of the temple and disappeared into the neighboring streets.

"Maybe we can get out now." Michael stood up and moved toward the door to the street. He pushed it open.

A woman frowned up at him from her cooking fire. Vegetables lay in a wicker basket next to a pot. On a nearby table, jugs of oil stood. Next to it a cauldron of water.

"Sorry." He closed the door again. "I guess we can't leave yet."

"Why are we even here?" Anne asked, but the answer did not come. She sat down and took Arthur on her lap, rocking him. The child closed his eyes.

Soon the men returned from the streets they'd dispersed along, now clean, dressed in soft wool robes, their wives and children following. They carried wine and food. Sang in gleeful voices.

Anne watched it all in amazement.

The door to the inner temple opened and a man in flowing blue and white robes walked out, looked around, then strode through the door to the outer enclosure. He continued through the next door and then disappeared down what Anne imagined was a set of stairs. Something about him nudged at her. Soon he appeared below at the door to the outer wall. He gathered his robes in one hand and headed out over the sand. He was walking toward them.

A nimbus of light surrounded his head and he wore a gold band on his head. His features became clearer as he came closer. Long flowing white hair to match his under robe. Gray streaked his beard. He had a noble brow with rounded eyes and a generous nose and mouth. The blue robe seemed to gleam with gemstones arranged in four rows of three each. Yet as he drew closer, she saw they were not there.

The man's hazel eyes lit with joy when he saw them and Anne's heart rose in her chest in delight. Michael stepped forward.

"Michael," the man called, using the Hebrew pronunciation. "There you are. We've been waiting for you."

"You've been . . . what?"

The man looked at Anne, then put his hand over his heart and gave a small bow. "Hannah? Shalom. You are the favored mother."

"I'm Anne," she said, "and you are?"

"My name is Melchizedek."

A gasp of surprise came from Michael. He fell to his knees. "Honored Wise One."

The high priest placed his hand on Michael's head as if in blessing, then said, "My son, this is unnecessary. You are one of my priests forever."

Michael pressed his forehead to the master's hand, then rose, his eyes filled with tears. He tried to speak, but seemed unable. He just shook his head.

"Yes, yes, it is good to see you as well." He helped Michael to his feet. "Now, where is the little one?"

Anne had also heard of the fabled master teacher

Melchizedek. She found her voice before her husband did. "Do you mean Arthur?"

"Yes, Aharon. You've given him the same name."

"But the first King Arthur hasn't been born yet." Now Michael's words came out all in a rush.

The priest waved this away with his hand as if it were inconsequential.

Arthur peeked around his mother at the tall man in flowing white and blue robes. Melchizedek knelt down and Arthur let go of his hold on Anne's jacket and walked up to the man.

"Hello," Arthur said.

"It is nice to see you, Aharon. Do you remember me?"

Arthur nodded solemnly.

Michael took another sharp breath in surprise.

"Jonathan needs our help. Do you think you could assist me?"

"Yes," Arthur said in his high child's voice.

"Good, let's go to the temple."

Arthur held his arms up, and the venerable high priest picked the child up and settled him on his hip. "Shall we?" Melchizedek looked behind him at Michael and Anne, then started to walk back the way he'd come.

Michael and Anne stepped out onto the sand and Uncle Ezra's shop melted away. They followed in the high priest's wake.

They reached the wall and two soldiers opened the doors for them. Anne caught up to Melchizedek and noticed Arthur was playing with the gemstones, now quite real, on the priest's breastplate.

"Arthur, leave those alone. They're very valuable."

Melchizedek smiled down at her, lighting her heart more. "The child is fine."

They climbed the steps and walked to the outer doors. Two soldiers came forward to bar Anne's way.

"The mother must also come," Melchizedek said.

They stepped back, allowing her to pass.

The group reached the door to the inner temple and the high priest gestured for Anne and Michael to walk in front of them. An attendant handed Anne a scarf of the same blue as Melchizedek's outer robe, only shot with streaks of silver. Michael squeezed her hand and she turned to see he was now dressed as a priest.

The high priest removed his sandals and indicated they should remove their shoes as well. Anne untied Arthur's small oxfords. Arthur held on to the edge of the high priest's blue robe, making the pomegranates and tiny golden bells tinkle.

She caught her breath when the doors to the Holy of Holies opened. A gold tiled floor stretched before them. Mid-way into the room, a square altar rose. A gold incense burner sat between two beeswax candles, their flames casting a glow. At the end of the room, seven steps led up to rich vermillion curtains trimmed in gold, now pulled closed. To the left stood a tall, gold lamp with small glass buds filled with yellow oil, three on each side, with a taller vial in the middle.

"Six for each point of the star," Melchizedek whispered to Arthur, who stood by his side, eyes wider than they had been in Rockefeller Square. "Do you remember what is in the middle?"

Arthur nodded sagely and pointed to his heart.

"That's my boy."

Priests came forward, lowering their heads to the master teacher. "Jonathan, you will serve as high priest here. We've come to rededicate the temple."

"Master, we only found one case of consecrated oil. The others have been fouled by the Syrians."

"I see. And you used this oil in the menorah."

"Yes, but it will take eight days to make more, and this light will go out."

"We will proceed."

The priests murmured amongst themselves, shaking their heads in worry, but took their places as instructed. Two moved forward and pulled back the crimson curtains. Behind it, two gold cherubim faced each other, their wings spread forward, on top of a gold box engraved with arcane symbols.

The Arc. Anne dropped to her knees.

The high priest began to chant, a sound that reached deep into her bones and vibrated her core. A sound that enlivened the walls of the temple. Soon the box began to glow.

Then Jonathan Maccabee knelt before Melchizedek and the high priest spoke more words that Anne could not make out. He anointed Jonathan with some oil, his forehead, throat, heart, hands, and feet.

One of the priests took a taper and lit it with one of the beeswax candles on the center altar. He carried it to Melchizedek, who took it and lit the wicks on the menorah. As he did so, he chanted under his breath and Arthur held out his hands, palms forward.

Melchizedek wet his fingers and put out the taper, then looked down at Arthur. "Thank you, my son. May you be blessed."

"Michael, where are you?" came a voice, and with it the scene faded. They found themselves standing in the middle of an antique jewelry store. The faint scent of dust and cinnamon reached Anne's nose.

The curtains in the back of the store opened and an older man with unruly hair wearing wire rim glasses came out. "There you are. We were worried."

"Uncle Ezra," Michael said.

"Come, come. It's almost sunset. We need to light the first

candle." He leaned down in front of Arthur. "Do you want to light the menorah, Aharon?"

"Lights," Arthur shouted enthusiastically.

They all laughed.

Arthur took his uncle's hand and they walked out into the hallway together. Ezra pushed the elevator button.

"Are you coming?" he shouted back at Anne and Michael.

"What just happened?" Anne asked.

"I have no idea," Michael said, "but we're back safe and sound."

"I'm getting hungry," Uncle Ezra called out.

"We're coming," Michael said.

And so Arthur helped light his second menorah of the evening and they feasted, talking and laughing. The older children played with the dreidel and Michael showed Anne the Hebrew letters on it.

"I'm sure there's a deeper meaning," she said.

"Yes, but that's enough for tonight, don't you think?"

She kissed his cheek. "Enough for tonight."

"Aw, the love birds. Are you thinking of giving me another grandchild?" Michael's mother teased.

The evening passed quickly. At last, Anne and Michael gathered up the sleeping Arthur and walked to the subway to head to their apartment in town. When they reached Rockefeller Square, the lights on the huge tree blazed and the angels stood guard, their trumpets ready to announce the birth of the Master Teacher.

Anne gave Arthur a gentle shake. "Wake up, sleepy head. See? The tree is lit up now."

Arthur lifted his head and reached out a chubby hand. "Lights, Mommy."

She kissed him in wonder. What other miracles would come?

A Star, A Star

The popular press was calling it the Christmas Star, the final powerful conjunction of 2020. Jupiter and Saturn joining together to create a bright star even rivaling brilliant Sirius. Some articles mentioned that it was occurring on Winter Solstice. At least it was winter in the northern hemisphere. Summer in the southern half of the world. Social media had done more to create a global society than any government, so Anne was always reminded of the polar opposite seasons by her friends down under and their trip to Peru.

The metaphysical world was all atwitter, calling this the beginning of the Aquarian Age, heralding a transformation of the world's governments and further opening of human consciousness. Grandmother Elizabeth had gathered the Isis Lodge together to celebrate the event. She invited Michael's group, Lodge Rose Croix, to join them at The Oaks, the Le Clair family's sprawling home in the New England countryside. Spouses, domestic partners, and children were also welcome. The Oaks would be full for the first time all year.

"Are you sure it's safe?" Anne asked her when she announced the plans.

"Winston has worked up a strict protocol," Grandmother Elizabeth explained. Dr. Winston Stuart was a nationally respected physician as well as a member of Isis Lodge. "Everyone is to isolate for two weeks before the event, take a test after the first week and again right before traveling. We'll arrange for transportation so we can be sure they're not exposed on the way here. Temperatures will be taken every morning and tests every two days. We've bought N95 masks for everyone."

"My goodness," Michael had said. "But some people have to work."

"We'll make up lost wages, but most are working remotely already. My secretary checked."

"That's a lot of effort."

But Grandmother Elizabeth only shrugged. "It's the beginning of a new age. We should mark it well."

"If you're sure it will be safe," Anne conceded. "We want you and Grandfather around a lot longer."

"I will stay to watch my grandson grow up," Grandmother Elizabeth declared.

Some people arrived the afternoon of December 20th and dinner was lively. The members of the two lodges sat with an empty place between them, masks off to eat. They enjoyed getting to know each other. Guy Allen, the astrologer from Michael's lodge, had regaled them with overwhelming detail about the progression of planetary encounters they'd been subject to this year.

"It's no wonder everything has practically shut down," he said. His enthusiasm sometimes involved spitting food when he talked with his mouth full. He was oblivious to Grandmother

Elizabeth's frowns. Anne bit her lip to keep from laughing, but she had to admit his account was fascinating.

"The world was forced to quiet down. To go into a more contemplative mode," he explained.

Winston raised a finger and Guy quieted. A Christmas miracle in Anne's opinion. "Except for the hospitals. Our staff has been worn down to a nub by it all."

"Yes, yes. It must be very sobering," Guy said, trying to look somber.

"Still, we know there is no death," Grandmother Elizabeth added. "Not of the soul. The many who have left are with us in another realm."

"Who?" Arthur asked from his highchair, looking around at the crowd.

The two grandparents' faces melted into adoring smiles. "No one here, darling. Now eat your peas."

"Peas, yuck." Arthur threw down his spoon in defiance.

Anne stifled another laugh. Then shook her head when Gerald, Arthur's grandfather, scooped up some peas.

"Peas are yummy." He aimed the spoon at Arthur's mouth. "Here comes here airplane."

Arthur screwed up his mouth and turned his head away.

"He'll eat if he's hungry. Or he'll starve," Anne said in her mother voice, shaking her head slightly.

Gerald put down the spoon and ostentatiously turned his head away from the child.

Guy picked up the conversation again, and with nobody paying Arthur any mind, the child started eating again.

The two grandparents were doing quite well with Arthur attending family meals more often. Their own children had been fed separately by the nannies. They were adapting to the change. After all, the Age of Aquarius was upon them, Anne thought.

"The Jyotish crowd insists we're still in Capricorn," Guy said.

"Jyotish?" someone asked from down the table.

"Vedic astrology. Given the precessions, they're right, but Western astrology always works better for me."

He started to go into detail about the dance of Saturn and Jupiter with Pluto over the year, but the grand matriarch raised her palm. "Mr. Allen. We all appreciate your obvious expertise, but we plan to explore all this in our temple teaching tomorrow. Let us not exhaust the subject over our meal."

"In the temple?" Guy asked, his eyes alight. "Will there be a drama?"

Grandmother Elizabeth's smile was Sphinx-like. "You will see, Mr. Allen. You will see."

The next afternoon found the group gathered in the Isis Temple, hidden away behind the grand ballroom. Chairs were set up in a semi-circle near the eastern entrance and a white sheet hung against the western wall. The family quartz ball still stood on its perch in the middle of the room.

"That is an impressive crystal," Stephen said, Michael's second in charge of Lodge Rose Croix.

"It is," Michael said. Seeing the fire in his friend's eye, he continued. "Maybe we can arrange for the lodge to have some time with it."

Stephen looked like he'd been given the best Christmas gift in his entire life. "Would you?"

Michael patted him on the shoulder. "I promise."

Grandmother Elizabeth cleared her throat and the murmured conversations stopped. "We're not going to do a formal working this afternoon. Rather we will watch a sacred drama reenacting the astrology of 2020." She went behind a group of partitions that had been set up on one side of the temple, almost like a dressing room.

The lights dimmed.

After a hushed silence, Gerald appeared dressed in a gray robe carrying a scythe and an hourglass.

"Granddaddy!" shouted Arthur.

"Let's listen," Michael whispered.

Images of the Saturn temple in Rome appeared on the sheet behind him. Anne turned and found David Wilt sitting behind a computer and some kind of projector.

"I am Cronos, known to you as Saturn. I was a Titan, child of the mother earth and sky father, Gaia and Uranus. We Titans created this world." Gerald spread his hands.

Anne held her breath, hoping he didn't drop any props.

"My children are Jupiter, Neptune, Pluto, Juno, Ceres and Vesta. I am lord of seasons and harvest. I keep the seed, watch the grain grow, and cut it down again." Gerald swept the scythe in front of his body.

Anne hoped the aluminum wrapped around the end would hold.

Images of waving grain played on the sheet in the background.

"I rule the tides of time and keep the law. If you disobey, I will restrict you."

"You devoured us," came another voice. It was Bill Hardy, another member of the lodge, dressed in a black robe with a helmet on his head and carrying a gold-covered shield. "Who kills his own children?"

"Pluto," Gerald cried out.

An image of the small planet shown on the back wall. Then a phoenix rising from a fire.

"You were rebellious. You all tried to usurp me." Arthur squirmed in Anne's lap.

"It's just pretend, sweetie."

"I wear the helmet of invisibility to hide from my enemies, you most of all. I carry with me the gold and riches of the underworld."

"I found you," Saturn said in a low, gravelly voice.

"I am the lord of death, but also rebirth and regeneration. We returned and exiled you."

"I created a Golden Age while away from Olympus."

As they spoke, the two walked closer and closer to each other.

"The tides of time shift. The time has come for change," declared Saturn.

"I am glad to hear it," Pluto said.

They stood together, arm in arm. "Together we will dismantle the old law," Grandfather Gerald declared. "The Golden Age will return."

The spotlight above them went out.

"The first conjunction in January." Another light revealed the speaker to be Grandmother Elizabeth dressed as Isis. "Time to shed the old. Close your eyes and remember what you have released in this last year."

After a minute of silence, somebody bumped against the partition separating the actors and the audience. Stephen jumped up and steadied it.

A spotlight went on and Winston Stuart walked onto the stage dressed in purple robes and carrying a thunderbolt.

"I am Zeus, the child who survived our father. You know me now as Jupiter."

The image of a majestic eagle played on the screen behind him, then the planet Jupiter filled the screen.

"I am expansion, healing, and prosperity. I push the boundaries out while our father Saturn constricts. I bring you luck and wealth."

Pluto returned to the stage. "Brother, I have met with our father and he says the time is drawing near to bring in a new age. A new law that respects the unique individual and celebrates equality."

As he spoke, the two moved closer and closer together.

"I am glad to hear it. Let us come together, then, to continue the destruction of the old order."

Grandmother Elizabeth walked on stage as the two planets came close together. "Jupiter and Pluto met three times this year to ensure the explosion of our old paradigm. Close your eyes and remember. What happened to you in April, the end of June, and the middle of November?"

The audience closed their eyes and each thought through the year, remembering the challenges, the changes, the losses and gains. Grandmother Elizabeth gave them a longer time to reflect.

Softly, a familiar tune began to play. As the volume gradually increased, Anne recognized the old song by the Fifth Dimension. The lyrics rang out. "It is the dawning of the Age of Aquarius, the Age of Aquarius. Aquarius."

Anne's mother, Katherine, jumped up. The song belonged to her generation. She held her arms out to her grandson. "Let's dance, Arthur."

Arthur reached up to her and she took him to the back of the temple and swayed to the music with him perched on her hip.

An image from The Lord of the Rings appeared on the screen behind the stage. Galadriel pouring water out of the large silver vessel into the basin that formed her mirror. Then the two wavy lines symbolizing Aquarius followed. Next, the constellation of the water bearer.

The spotlights switched on again. Saturn came onto the stage. "I arrived in Aquarius first."

Guy was squirming in his chair, a look of delight on his face. Anne thought it was all a little hokey.

Jupiter came out next. "I arrived two days later."

The spotlight brightened.

They joined hands. "And tonight, we will turn the tides. The world will swing into the new age."

Saturn held up his scythe. "The old order will crumble."

Jupiter held up his thunderbolt. "The new light will strike us all."

The lights in the temple went up. Grandmother Elizabeth appeared dressed in her ordinary clothes. "Let us all go and witness the new beginning."

The group filed out to the ballroom where they found the French doors thrown open. They walked out onto the lawn and milled about, laughing and chatting.

Low clouds had banked the southwest earlier in the day. Anne hoped they'd clear and give them at least a peek.

Gerald appeared, the last of his costume shed, and led them all to a path that wound through the garden and out to a high point in the horse pastures that faced southwest. The animals were all in the stable for the night.

Members of the staff handed out blankets to sit on and wool wraps. Katherine deposited a sleeping Arthur in Anne's arms. Honestly, he was getting heavy. She walked out and found a spot on the hillside. She settled down with the sleeping child. Michael sat next to her in silence. He took Arthur and laid him down, swaddling him in with a wool poncho they'd bought in Peru.

Anne squinted at the southwestern horizon, willing the last clouds to clear. Her eyes strayed higher, marking the brightest star in the sky. Sirius pierced the velvet dark. Now she thought of it as Michael's star because of the crystal key he carried.

It reminded her of their adventure in Peru. How the crystal key holders had been called by the Inca to do ritual for the turning of the Mayan calendar and the return of Los Viejos, the Old Ones.

Behind Sirius sprawled the three bright points of Orion's belt. Such a beautiful constellation, but its native crystal held so much darkness. She wondered if this would change now. The Seven Sisters clustered like a dim egg, the individual stars impossible to distinguish with the naked eye, at least tonight.

Michael stuck his hand down to her. She grasped it and he pulled her to her feet. She brushed dry grass off her jeans, then pointed up at the sky. "There they are. The homes of our progenitors. At least some of them."

He put his arm around her shoulder and pulled her close.

She nestled against him. "They all showed up. All the Old Ones, but it feels like a dream."

"Uh huh," he said, so low it sounded like the deep purr of a jaguar.

"It's always like that," she said in a quiet voice. "When we come home from these adventures, I wonder if it all really happened."

Michael squeezed her shoulder. "It did. I remember it, too. And everyone else who went with us."

A sudden gasp rose from the group of people strewn out along the hillside in front of them. Several arms rose to point. There, low on the horizon, the two planets blazed out, looking for all the world like one star.

"There they are," Michael said.

"Welcome, Christmas Star," Grandmother Elizabeth called out.

Others joined her, some calling out the new age.

Katherine started to sing, "When the moon is in the seventh house."

"Except it's not," Guy corrected in a whisper. He was next to them, binoculars to his face.

Then the group spontaneously sang the chorus of the Christmas carol. "A star, a star, dancing in the night. He will bring us goodness and light."

They'd mixed up the verses, but Anne smiled, looking up at the winking planets dancing so close the naked eye could not separate them out.

The tail was not as big as a kite, but it would do. It would do.

Cup o' Kindness

Anne Le Clair snuggled under Michael's arm, stifling a yawn. They watched the television tuned to Times Square, waiting for the ball to drop. It used to be easy to sit up until midnight on New Year's Eve, but she'd stuffed herself to the gills on Estelle's feast.

She glanced at the grandfather clock in the corner. Two more minutes. Anne took in the sight of all the crystal holders and the people who'd helped them with their adventures gathered together around the tree, chatting quietly. They'd spent the day talking off and on, trying to figure out if their duties were over.

Thirty seconds until the New Year. She stood and raised her glass of sparkling water, the only thing she could drink at the moment.

The countdown sounded on the television. *Ten, nine.*

"Crystal holders, our magical helpers, those who kept us safe." She nodded to people in each of these categories as she named them. "We have successfully ushered in the Awakening."

They all raised their glasses, if they had them. If not, a hand. Tahir threw some confetti into the air. She had no idea where he found it.

Three, two, Happy New Year.

"Happy New Year," everyone shouted at once.

Anne kissed Michael, then Tahir's cheek.

"To the Awakening!" she shouted.

"The Awakening," the group echoed.

And that's when it happened.

Anne's holiday season had been especially busy this year with the virus under control at last. Hannukah had come early, so they spent two days with Michael's family, lighting candles, opening gifts, watching the children all play together. Arthur adored the crowd of cousins, aunts, uncles and proud grandparents.

Next came Grandmother Elizabeth's annual gala for the family's outer circle—important families, business owners, politicians. Her grandmother had skipped it last year, breaking a two hundred year tradition. With a former president and current U.S. Senator, it was important to keep the family's connections lively. The Oaks had overflowed with people, food, and drink. Anne remembered when she'd worn the crystal pendant openly, defiantly, when she first inherited the stone and the dressing down by her grandmother she received.

Then on Solstice night, the inner circle celebrated with a formal ritual. Their magical group had grown substantially since the crystals had become active again, combining Grandmother's Isis Lodge with Michael's Rose Croix circle, and Valentin Knight's highly esteemed Lodge of Melchizedek. The ceremony had been a powerhouse, lifting her into that luminous awareness she'd experienced a few times in their adventures, the one she both yearned for and doubted was real when she returned to her more ordinary self.

The extended family stayed to celebrate Christmas, the noise and exchanging of news firmly grounding Anne in ordinary life again. Her cousin Christine recently gave birth to a girl, her second child, and brought the baby along husband and slightly older son, who was Arthur's age. Their very own U.S. Senator, Uncle Philip, arrived the next day with his whole brood. Both his grown children had young ones. The Oaks filled up.

An ecstatic Arthur showed all his cousins around, solemnly introducing them to each of the horses by name, coaxing the now grown Iset out of hiding, and playing with the new dog. Rainey had shown up with her and three puppies a couple of months ago. The mom was dubbed Anput after the wife of Anubis, but the puppies were given Celtic names after the mythic dogs Cú Chulainn, Bran, and Sceolan. Michael told the stories to Arthur at bedtime, but Anne couldn't remember it all.

Arthur couldn't pronounce any of their names, and neither could she, if truth be told, so he made up his own. The names changed from day to day, so Anne had given up keeping track. She just hoped the dogs weren't too confused by it. But they adored Arthur, ran to him when he appeared near the barn and rough housed to his heart's delight. Miraculously, he escaped the melee with only minor scratches.

Christmas morning, Arthur snuck into their bedroom with a pack of giggling cousins all set to awaken the adults, violating the wait-until-six-o'clock edict. Estelle, the cook, had been no help at all, serving the children hot cider and German sugar cake before they raided all their parents' bedrooms. Present opening was early and riotous, leaving everyone knee deep in wrapping paper and dodging screeching children debating who'd gotten the very best toy.

At last it was New Year's Eve. Grandmother Elizabeth said this year she was throwing another party. A special event. She invited the crystal holders and all the people who'd helped over the years to celebrate their success. Anne just hoped her grandmother was right. That they'd been successful and they were safe from those bent on perpetuating darkness.

Yesterday, Tahir Nur Ahram walked through the front doors of The Oaks and dropped his gym bag on the Italian tile. Anne stifled a laugh. One day she'd learn to travel as light as he did.

"Michael," Tahir called out, opening his arms wide. Michael stepped into a huge hug.

Next in line to greet Tahir, Anne offer her hand to shake, but he gathered her into a big bear hug. As soon as she moved back, Jerome, their butler, took Tahir's bag. "I can show you to your room, sir, if you'd like to freshen up."

Jerome started up the stairs, but Tahir stood in the foyer taking it all in. At last, he said, "Nice house," and followed the butler up the stairs.

Maria graciously accepted a ride on the family jet, arriving from Guatemala City a few hours after Tahir's plane landed. Tahir had steadfastly refused their offer to buy him a ticket. Annoyingly stubborn as always. Anne would find a way to repay him without offending his pride. Two crystal holders were missing. Yeshe, the Tibetan nun who seemed to be the true holder of the Antares stone. Nobody could figure out how to send her an invitation. Except maybe just thinking about it. Lord Daniel Stainton, the Orion crystal holder, had not been invited because he was probably still a dark magician. Although Anne wasn't entirely sure he still held the stone.

As the early darkness settled around the oaks lining the

front drive and the horses headed in from the pastures, their blankets gathering damp, the family and staff lit the multitude of candles. The crystal holders and their friends gathered in the living room where the tall Douglas fir still twinkled in the corner. The Le Clairs followed the old ways, removing holiday decorations after Twelfth Night. The children had been fed and sent to play in one of the apartments upstairs under the watchful eye of Rebecca and two more nannies. Just adults tonight.

Estelle appeared, a bit breathless from the last minute rush in the kitchen. "May I have your attention?"

Conversation lulled as the group turned to the family chef.

"I don't know the whole story, but I wanted to honor all of you who saved the world from darkness over these last few years—" she blushed, then stammered out "—and that is no exaggeration, I'm told."

"Oh, Estelle—" Anne began.

"I'm not finished, dear," she interrupted with a firm nod. "You have risked your lives against what evil I do not know. We lost our Thomas and Cynthia. Then Bob, who taught our boy to drive. What a rascal he was." She shook her head.

They waited while she wiped a tear from her cheek. She squared her shoulders. "But we gained Michael and our Arthur was saved with the help of all of you, especially Mr. Knight. So, this meal is in honor of you all."

She went back into the kitchen. The temporary wait staff she'd hired for the evening appeared and began circulating with trays of hors d'oeurvres. Figs stuffed with goat cheese and honey, brie with cranberries spread on crackers, dates, and plant-based salami caprese skewers. Anne tried to just nibble because she'd seen the crates and boxes being delivered to the kitchen over the last few days. Christmas dinner had been a tour de force, but this meal promised to outshine it. She didn't know where Estelle got her energy.

Estelle had worked all week, ordering in from Scotland, France, even Japan. In the last two days, she'd chased everyone out of the kitchen. Except Arthur, who sat eating scones, overseeing the proceedings like the king he used to be, until Anne sent him off say goodbye to his cousins. The menu was as carefully guarded as a state secret. Arthur was too young to spill the beans.

Anne made her way around the room, being sure everyone had something to drink, enough napkins, answering any questions, even though the staff was doing a great job. She just needed to connect with everyone. She saw Dr. Abernathy standing next to the large fireplace watching with a bemused expression and joined him.

They shared a minute of quiet companionship for a minute, then Anne asked the question that was really on her mind. "Is Estelle right? Is it really over?"

The recent descendant of the Templar knight who'd been assigned to protect the bloodline studied her, his eyes sharp as an eagle's. "I can't say. It would seem the arrival of the enlightened ones at the end of the ceremony might signal the end of the transition."

"I only caught a glimpse of them before—" Anne waved her hand in the air "—before whatever it was happened. How can we know for sure?"

"You have doubts?" he asked.

Anne tried to find the right words, but before she could answer him, Jerome arrived in the doorway. He bowed to Grandmother Elizabeth. "Dinner is served."

They found their names on little cards sitting on a pile of plates that promised entirely too many courses. Grandmother Elizabeth and her husband Gerald took their seats at each end of the table and with a loud scrapping of chairs, the rest of them sat.

The waiters appeared and placed a mushroom spinach salad in front of each person. People chatted, but chewing soon replaced serious conversation. Next came a Scottish salmon linguine. The vegetarian option swam with capers and red peppers. The fish melted in Anne's mouth. She swallowed her doubts along with the delicious cream sauce.

As the plates were cleared, Maria looked around at the group, then at Anne, a question in her eyes. "Everyone knows. We can talk frankly after—"Anne waved her hand absently, indicating the extra help.

Maria waited for the room to clear, then said, "We all made it home with our crystals. What do you think happened to Lord Stainton? Do you think he still has the last crystal?"

The Orion stone. The restless one, first held by Paul Marchand, whose hubris had led to his death in Egypt. Then controlled by Illuminati master Alexander Cagliostro, who'd mysteriously disappeared in Glastonbury. Somehow found by Nina Lockhart, who'd kidnapped Valentin Knight. After her death, her family had sold the necklace, unaware of its importance. The last holder was Lord Stainton, who'd disappeared in the overwhelming rush of light and energy in Peru that had swept them all away.

"Did that really happen?" Anne asked.

Michael set his wine glass down. "Did what happen?"

Anne looked around at the rest of the people who'd been in Peru. "You know, the whole thing in Peru. I mean, we woke up on the floor of the barn of all places."

"Me, too." Michael and Arnold said at the same time.

Rainey caught Anne's eye and nodded.

"Was it all a dream?" she asked.

"Not if we all remember it. I was returned to my bed in Giza," Tahir said.

"I found myself in a temple up the hill from my village," Maria said.

Before they could say more, Jerome ushered in the helpers carrying the *pièces de resistance*, a plethora of offerings. Duck confit served with roasted potatoes, polenta with roasted mushrooms and thyme, Brussels sprouts with a balsamic glaze, green beans with roasted almonds. Anne couldn't take it all in. They'd have to carry her off for sure.

Everyone filled their plates and began to taste Estelle's magic, the questions put on hold for the moment. But after they'd sated their appetites, conversation started up again.

Rainey cleared her throat. Everyone stared at her. She never spoke. "If you don't mind me asking, what exactly happened before we were transported home? Strange beings came through the portal. I heard murmurings in my mind, but couldn't make out what was being said."

Anne realized she was staring and gave herself a shake. "Once we leave a ceremony, I find my clarity fades. I can't remember it all. Only bits and pieces."

Maria took a sip of water. "I believe the star elders who brought the crystals to earth originally returned that night."

"Relatives of Akhenaton," Tahir mused. "They seemed to have elongated skulls."

"I saw a cat with wings," Michael said.

"Rainey," Anne said. "If I remember correctly, you seemed to recognize the being who came through at the end."

The mysterious woman smiled Sphinx-like. "Yes, I've spent time in the east with Buddhists."

Anne noticed she'd revealed nothing about where or what kind of Buddhists.

"I believe we may have witnessed the return of the Maitreya Buddha," Rainey said.

Michael half stood, jostling the table. "The Master Teacher?"

"Who?" Tahir put down his napkin. "I am not well versed in Eastern traditions."

Everyone's eyes turned to Rainey, but she nodded for Michael to explain. "The Maitreya Buddha is said to be the next enlightened teacher of the Aquarian Age."

"Holy cow," Anne said, then blushed. What an inadequate reaction. "But it's been almost a year and we've heard nothing more."

"If he has arrived, though," Tahir said, "perhaps we have succeeded. Perhaps your cook is correct."

"Dessert is served," Jerome's deep bass voice started them. No one had heard him arrive.

The chandelier was extinguished, leaving the soft glow of the tapers illuminating their faces. A brighter glow approached from the hallway. Four waiters came into the room rolling a serving cart. In the middle sat an enormous cake ablaze with candles. Estelle came in behind it. "Would all the crystal holders come forward, please?"

Anne glanced at Michael, who shrugged. The four of them gathered around the cake.

"Make a wish for the birth of the new year," Estelle instructed.

Honestly, their chef was turning into a mystic, Anne thought. She'd certainly been with them long enough.

"On the count of three," Michael said. He nodded for Gerald to do the countdown. They all took a huge breath and on three, blew with all their might.

The group applauded loudly. A few candles flickered in the middle. Michael leaned over and blew the rest out.

Estelle took up a large knife from the cart and handed it, handle first, to Grandmother Elizabeth. "If you'd do the honors."

Laughing, the matriarch said, "I can only make the first cut. Your experts here can serve."

They somehow found room for a few bites of chocolate cake, as light as the heart weighed by Anubis against a feather supplied by Ma'at. Hazelnut mousse oozed from the middle layers and the frosting seemed to be chocolate ganache. The waiters spooned fresh raspberries and blueberries onto each slice and topped each with a dollop of whipped cream.

I'll never walk again, Anne thought.

After dessert, the waiters poured digestifs and Anne drank the Amaro Montenegro, hoping it would make some headway in cutting through the heavy meal.

Then the group moved on to the ballroom where the life-size frieze still sat. Anne noticed Michael looking carefully at the alabaster jar held by the third wise man. The two thousand year old alabaster jar.

Michael found Anne's eyes smiled at her. Anne had sent him on a treasure hunt his first Christmas at The Oaks. And he'd found the artifact. They both watched the others, wondering who would notice it.

Grandfather Gerald read the passage from the King James version of the Bible about the night of the nativity, then more about the arrival of the wise men. "These sacred teachers arrived near Epiphany, the end of the twelve days of Christmas. If what we have heard tonight is true, the next World Teacher has arrived. This one fully grown."

"Let's hope so," Anne whispered in Michael's ear.

Gerald glanced at his old fashioned wristwatch. "We have ten minutes before midnight. Shall we adjourned to the living room to watch the ball drop?"

People got to their feet and moved toward the door.

"What ball?" Tahir asked.

Maria came up behind him. "Ball drop? Is there a football game at midnight?"

Laughing, Anne explained the tradition of lowering a glowing ball in Times Square, counting down the last seconds of the year. When they arrived in the living room, the waiters were handing out glasses of champagne. Anne and Tahir both asked for sparking water.

They gathered around the television, some lounging on the couches, chatting together.

Thirty seconds until the New Year. Anne stood and raised her glass of sparkling water, the only thing she could drink at the moment.

The countdown sounded on the television. *Ten, nine.*

"Crystal holders, our magical helpers, those who kept us safe." She nodded to people in each of these categories as she named them. "We have successfully ushered in the Awakening."

Why not declare it? she thought.

They all raised their glasses, if they had them. Tahir threw some confetti into the air. She had no idea where he found it.

Three, two, Happy New Year, the television announced.

"Happy New Year," everyone shouted at once.

Anne kissed Michael, then Tahir's cheek.

"To the Awakening!" she shouted.

"The Awakening," the group echoed.

"We'll take a cup o' kindness yet," Anne sang.

The rest joined in, "To Auld Lang Syne."

And then it happened.

Suddenly, the light in the room shifted and a breeze started up from somewhere. Anne knew the windows were all closed. Startled, everyone moved away from a growing ball of light that had suddenly appeared in the center of the room.

Something tickled Anne's memory. Yes, Egypt. At the last minute, the Tibetans had stepped through a portal of light bringing the sixth crystal to the ceremony, completing the magic. A portal of light like the one forming in the middle of The Oaks' living room.

The light grew almost too bright to look at. The scent of ozone wafted from the swirling globe. Then a subtle chime sounded, the globe stabilized, and Yeshe stepped out.

"Yes, to the Awakening. But first we're going to need your help."

A Merry Buddhist Christmas

P rium opened the back of his battered Toyota truck so air could flow through. He didn't want Frederick to get overheated while he laid out the grid. He grabbed up the ropes and stakes, then walked down the faint footpath in the jungle until he reached the end. Using the metal detector, he pushed the vegetation away, looking for any gleam of steel. This was the most dangerous part of the job. The detectors weren't as good as the rats. They missed mines that were buried just a little too deep. His friend Sov had missed a landmine and lost a leg just a month ago.

Prium drove the first stake and fed the guiding rope through the first loop, then crept along, sweeping the metal detector before him like the grass trimmers they used at the fancy hotels. He drove the second stake, fed the rope through, and continued until he'd marked out a good run.

He returned to the vehicle and put Frederick into his harness. Frederick was an African giant pouched rat born and trained in Tanzania to sniff out explosives. About the size of a cat, his coat was the color of a malva nut, his underbelly the soft white of a lotus. Prium smiled at his thoughts. He'd grown quite fond of Frederick.

The rat gave out a little squeak when he saw his handler reach for his leash. Prium attached it to his harness and lifted the little guy to his shoulder where he rode as they walked back to the site. Prium hoped they'd find a few mines today. It was close to the end of the month and he could use the bonus if he went over his quota.

They reached the first stake and Prium attached Frederick's leash to the rope. The loops in the stakes were fashioned to allow the leash to pass through. Frederick gave an excited shrill and started off on his hunt. Prium squatted down and watched from a safe distance. The rat was light enough not to trigger the landmine. He would sniff it out, dig a little to uncover the metal if it wasn't on the surface, then squeak to his handler, expecting his reward. Frederick loved his treats—nuts, fruit, even lean meat—but grapes were his favorite. Prium had found some at headquarters today and grabbed them up.

The world had nicknamed them Hero Rats. Defusing landmines was the easy part. Finding them was tough. The Hero Rats did a great job finding explosive ordinances left behind by three decades of war. The website with pictures of their rats and a few people who'd lost limbs in explosions brought in good donations, which was vital. The rats cost a few thousand American dollars each due to their extensive training.

Frederick gave a series of squeaks, indicating he'd found something. They could generally sniff the high explosive inside the mine, but sometimes they just turned up discarded farm tools or guns from the war. Prium made his way over to Frederick, careful to step on ground the rat had already gone over. Frederick sat up on his haunches and reached out for his treat. Prium gave him a couple of grapes and knelt down to flag the find. But instead of a mine, a chunk of metal stuck out from the ground, engraved with something that looked old.

Prium gently moved dirt away from the piece, more and more of the flat disk coming visible. He loosened it from the ground and carefully lifted it, looking underneath for wires or a hidden explosive. Once he was certain it was safe, he pulled the disk out. Frederick sat watching. Prium gave the rat the signal to continue his search, then carried the disk back to the truck. He perched on the passenger seat, legs on the running board, and picked up a brush. He started to clean debris from the engraving. The top revealed a crown with a lotus flower at the top and circles inside sweeping wings rising up on both sides. This could be something ancient. A face from a lost temple. Valuable.

Excited, Prium kept brushing debris away, forcing himself to go slow. He couldn't risk damaging this artifact. Beneath the crown were three rows of petals with soil embedded in the crevices. He'd wait to get this out. He moved down to the face. Who would it be? Buddha? An old deva? Two lumps formed the forehead and the eyebrows swept away from a smaller lump in the middle that might have been another lotus at some point. Beneath this were round, upturned eyes, a large nose and frowning mouth. An asura. He'd found an old carving of a demon just like the ones on the bridge into Angkor Tom.

Prium blew on the face to clear it off. The metal disk started to hum.

Except that wasn't possible.

He checked his radio, but it was off. No panels on the dashboard were lit up. Patting his pocket, he felt the lump of the keys. He looked around, but saw nothing but the green of fig trees and a stand of magnolia bushes.

The humming stopped.

Had he imagined it?

Prium turned the disk and shook more dirt off, then put it back on his lap and brushed his hand over it. He leaned closer to study the face.

The eyes opened.

He gasped, his breath heavy.

Nothing happened. He let out his breath with a sigh.

The hum returned, louder this time. The disk began to vibrate.

With a shout, Prium threw it away, but instead of falling, it hovered in front of him for a few seconds, then shot into the sky.

Two Months Later

Anne Le Clair tilted her head toward the interpreter as he translated the monarch's speech. Michael Levy leaned toward him as well. The man kept his voice soft, for their ears only. He didn't want to insult His Majesty by talking too loudly. Cambodia's king was elected and, much like the United Kingdom, didn't have much administrative power. He was more of a figurehead representing peace, stability, and prosperity. His speech reflected this status. As he dedicated a newly excavated temple in the sprawling complex in Siem Reap, he spoke of restoring honor for the ancient heritage of the Khmer people

Grandmother Elizabeth had asked Anne to go to the dedication in her stead, claiming she was now too old to travel halfway across the globe. The family contributed heavily to foundations committed to archaeological research and restoration of ancient sites. "The knowledge is there," Grandmother Elizabeth said, "carved on the walls, embedded in the sacred geometry of the structures. This type of work is part of our responsibility."

Anne had honored the country at last night's reception by wearing a traditional silk dress and heavily embroidered collar, all stitched with the gold silk that was Cambodia's national thread. The king's eyes had lit up with appreciation for her thoughtfulness. Today's speech marked the end of the ceremonies.

She and Michael had come a week early, not announcing their arrival so they could be free. He'd explored the ruins of the area and sated his archaeological curiosity. Anne had enjoyed the peace of the place, but not experienced any visions or psychic revelations. After a week of climbing temples and poking through the roots of fig trees at more distant sites, balancing on fallen stone, they attended the formal events. Both she and Michael were eager to get home. Christmas was a week away and they still needed to finish shopping.

After lots of bows over hands folded together and assurances of more support from the foundation she was representing, Anne and Michael were escorted to a waiting car. Anne slid across the back seat with Michael following. She let out a big sigh of relief.

"Glad it's all over?" Michael asked.

"Yes, I'm ready to go home and see Arthur. He grows so fast, we might not recognize him."

Michael chuckled. Arnold, the head of family security, got in the front seat. They wound through town, enjoying the sparkle of the river next to the street, the tuk-tuks, the press of people. The car soon pulled into the grounds of their hotel and rounded the circular drive. A hotel porter ran to open the door and escort them inside where they were greeted once again by the enormous Christmas tree in the center of the lobby. Carols played loudly from speakers that seemed to be positioned everywhere.

They'd been curious to travel to a mostly Buddhist country during the holiday to experience something different than the deluge of Santas, Christmas trees, reindeer, and lights that had been up since early November, so they'd been dismayed to find that Cambodia had dressed up for the holiday just like America. At least their hotel did. "Silent Night" played softly and Anne knew that "We Three Kings" would come next. Unfortunately, she'd memorized the order of the carols.

A family stood in front of the tree posing for the camera. Their tour guide had explained that people drove up from Phnom Penh to see this novel holiday display. Anne headed toward the stairwell while Michael tipped the footman. Chairs and sofas clustered in groups in the massive lobby. Once she cleared the tree and large Santa that looked suspiciously like Buddha beneath his red hat, she spotted something in an alcove that stopped her in her tracks.

Yeshe, the Tibetan nun they'd met in Peru, the one who'd stepped through a portal last New Year's Eve and told them she needed their help, sat watching her. Beside her was Tahir, Michael's Egyptian teacher. Behind them stood Rainey, Yeshe's security, the woman who Anne secretly suspected of being an assassin and an even deeper secret, Arnold's girlfriend.

Michael barreled up to her and almost ran into her still form. "Let's get to our room so we can—" He'd spotted them. "Tahir?"

Arnold ran to them, then stopped when he saw everyone else. His mouth dropped. Anne noticed a smile ghost over Rainey's mouth. They were definitely a couple.

"We have a situation," Yeshe said.

Anne, Michael, and Arnold stood speechless for a few seconds. Then they all spoke at once.

"But we were just leaving—" Anne blurted out.

"How did you get here?" Michael was talking to Tahir.

Lead us to thy perfect light rang out from the loudspeakers.

Anne rolled her eyes at the hint from the universe.

"What do you need?" Arnold asked.

"Yes," Anne said, "How can we help?"

A group of solemn Chinese tourists walked by, mostly in a line. Yeshe eyed them, waiting for them to pass. "Follow us," Michael said. "We have a suite."

They headed to the elevators, Michael and Tahir's heads together as usual as they started to catch up on news. The security team fell into position, Arnold taking the lead with Rainey walking behind them. Did they really think there was danger here? Anne wondered.

Arnold opened the double doors to their rooms and asked them to wait while he did a quick security sweep. He waved them in and they spread themselves around on the low sofas and comfy chairs clustered in the middle of the sitting area. A wide wall of windows looked out over the garden in the courtyard of the hotel. Over the fronds of several tall palms beyond the hotel walls, the green of the forest spread toward the temple area.

Anne jumped up again. "I'm forgetting my manners. What can I get you to drink? Are you hungry?"

Yeshe waved this away. "Business first."

Anne sat back down and faced the Tibetan nun, whose expression was more grave than she'd ever seen it.

"A month or two ago, we're not certain of the exact time, an ancient artifact was discovered."

Michael sat forward, always eager to hear about archaeological finds. "Is it valuable?"

Yeshe frowned. "It is dangerous."

Tahir nodded his agreement.

"You have your crystal keys with you?" she asked.

Anne lifted her pendant from beneath the white silk blouse she'd worn to the ceremony. Michael simply nodded.

"Excellent. I'll explain on the way. Our warriors are waiting." Yeshe stood, ready to go.

"Excuse me for asking, but could we change?" Anne asked. "We just got back from—"

"Yes, yes. Five minutes. Dress warm," Yeshe shouted after them.

Anne rushed into their bedroom and pulled pants and a cotton blouse from her almost packed suitcase. Michael did the same on the other side of the enormous bed. They'd been ready to leave. Their plane had already registered a flight plan.

"Did she say warriors?" Michael asked once they shut the door.

"I think so. What's happening?"

"Who knows." Michael pulled off his tux jacket. He didn't bother unfastening the shirt, but the buttons survived, much to Anne's amazement.

"We didn't bring warm clothes," Anne said, scrounging around for a sweater or jacket. She'd been taking at least two showers a day even in December with the heat and humidity in Cambodia.

"We'll figure it out." Michael headed for the door.

Back in the sitting area, Arnold and Rainey were checking their weapons, stowing various knives and guns in secret pockets and shoulder harnesses. "We need to call the pilot to reschedule," Anne told Arnold.

"It's already done," he said.

They all turned to Yeshe who took a firm stance, spread her arms, palms out, and began an incantation. Realizing she was going to open a portal right in the middle of the suite, Anne rushed to put the Do Not Disturb sign on the door and returned just as a golden circle formed in front of the dining room table. Yeshe continued her chant and the light from the circle intensified. A chime sounded and the portal snapped into place.

Yeshe nodded to Rainey. "You first."

Rainey stepped through, the rest following close behind. This time Arnold took up the rear. Anne couldn't resist closing her eyes and holding her breath when she went through these gateways. She always felt as if she were walking into a waterfall. The surface rippled like a lake and flicks of aquamarine moved through the gold light, just like a swimming pool in the noonday sun. She felt the shift when she reached the other side. Her ears popped, as if she'd gone up in altitude. She opened her eyes to a snow-capped mountain.

"This way." Yeshe moved off without looking behind to see if they followed.

They scrambled after her down a hallway open to the mountains on one side, the ancient stone wall of the structure on the other. The flagstones were mostly even beneath their feet, but an edge here and there demanded their eyes return to the floor even when the vistas called for their attention. Monks in saffron and red cīvaras moved quietly, turning to the side and bowing their heads to allow Yeshe and her group to pass.

Anne reached for Michael's hand and squeezed it for reassurance. "Where do you think we are?"

"Based on their robes, I'd say Tibet, but exactly which monastery, I haven't a clue."

They reached a flight of steps, narrow and steep. Anne gasped for air halfway up, the thin air a challenge. They reached the top and moved into an open courtyard. Anne leaned over, hands on her thighs, and panted until she caught her breath. Out of the corner of her eyes, she saw Arnold and Rainey, nonplussed, waiting politely. She'd been running regularly, blast them. Michael's red face reassured her that she wasn't the only one feeling the altitude. Tahir was the last to arrive. He held up a hand, not able to speak.

After another minute, Anne lifted her head and took in their surroundings. A statue of the Buddha dominated the center of the open area, rising at least twelve feet above her head. Pots of flowers and herbs sat around, dry stalks in the winter weather. A blast of air penetrated the jacket Anne had found at the bottom of her suitcase. Her eyes watered in the cold.

Yeshe gave them another minute to recover, then led them through a rounded archway and down another corridor that ended in red double doors decorated in elaborate gold filigree. Two goddess figures stood in the center of each door, one palm out. Anne wondered if they were supposed to stop negative energy from entering. Faint sounds of chanting reached them. Two men with curved swords in their hands nodded to the nun and opened the doors. Yeshe moved inside, the others on her heels.

Braziers set at either side of the entrance to the long hall blasted heat. Anne's shoulders relaxed as her body warmed. The vivid colors of the pillars and walls screamed out after the monochromatic white and gray of the mountains. Yeshe left them little time to take in the white tile floor decorated with gold knots, the red pillars and turquoise to deep blue ceilings, all painted with intricate gold symbols. The faces of various Buddhas and Taras watched impassively from the thangkas hanging on the walls. The heads of the monks lifted as Yeshe swept by, some expressions revealing concern, even fear.

What was happening here, Anne wondered. Palpable tension lay under the peaceful sound of the chants. The man sitting on a cushion at the end of the line of monks gestured for

Yeshe. He stood as she approached, his red and gold robes blending with the temple walls and columns.

Yeshe bowed over her pressed palms. "Abbot Choki."

"They are here?" he asked. A monk had stepped up to translate the Tibetan the two spoke.

"We have four sacred keys," Yeshe said.

The abbot nodded, his eyes lined, mouth tight with worry. "We will speak in my private study." He walked to a door in the back of the temple and opened it. The group followed and found themselves in a snug room. The back wall was filled with bookshelves holding old rolled scrolls and books. Zafu cushions lay in a semi-circle. The abbot folded himself up on one and with an outstretched hand invited them all to sit.

Tahir let out a grunt as he settled. At Michael's glance, he whispered, "Knees. I'm getting old."

Yeshe snorted at this. "We will get you some salve. This is Abbot Choki, as you no doubt heard." She'd switched to English. The translator moved just behind the abbot and began whispering in his ear. "I'll tell you as much as we know."

The door opened and two monks came in with a tray of tea. At Yeshe's direction, they put the tray on the worn rug in front of the group and left with a few too many bows in Anne's opinion. She picked up the cast iron tea pot and poured, then passed the delicate ceramic cups around as Yeshe explained.

"A week ago, Abbot Choki was hosting the ancient teacher who came to us in Peru. A man who appeared to be a powerful monk came to celebrate the return of this teacher. But he was an asura—" she caught Anne's look of confusion "—an ancient sorcerer, a demon."

"Thank you," Anne said. She supposed demons were real considering all she'd seen since inheriting the crystal key, although most of the evil had come from humans. She set down the warm tea pot reluctantly. This room had no heat. Apparently these monks kept themselves warm through some kind of mental discipline. She picked up her teacup and nursed in this spark of heat.

Yeshe continued. "The demon's name is Krong Reap and ages ago, he kidnapped Neang Seda, the shakti or wife as you say of Lord Preah Ream. They were wandering in the forest together where a jealous mother had exiled this true heir for ten years. His wife and Preah Ream's brother, Preah Leak, accompanied him."

She waved her hand. "It's a long story, but Krong fell in love with Seda and kidnapped her."

"Wait, isn't this the story of the Ramayana?" Michael asked, then hunched his shoulders when he realized he'd interrupted.

"Yes, in India this history is known by that title."

"But the names are different."

"I'm telling the Cambodian version since the demon came back to life from there," she explained.

'There.' She said 'there.' So we're not in Cambodia anymore, Anne thought.

"It's a myth, though," Tahir objected.

Yeshe shook her head. "It's history—all true. At any rate, Rama or Preah Ream, finally killed Krong Reap—"

Michael snapped his fingers. "Ravana. That's the demon's name."

Yeshe huffed in irritation and Rainey took a step toward her. Yeshe favored Michael with a long suffering look. "Yes, Krong Reap is Ravana, Rama is Preah Ream, Neang Seda is Sita, and Preah Lead is Lakshmana. Is everyone up to speed, as you say in America?"

Michael bowed his head. "I apologize for my impertinence, Lama Yeshe."

Yeshe sipped her tea and waited for everyone to settle

down. "This time Krong Reap has kidnapped the Maitreya Buddha."

"What?"

"How could he—"

"But is that even possible?"

The abbot held up a finger and spoke, the translator repeating in his heavily accented English. "He came among us well disguised. We detected his magic too late to stop him. But with your keys, we shall prevail and recover the promised one."

A chill spread through Anne, not from the snow-clad mountains around her this time, but from simple fear. Yeshe expected them to go up against some reanimated sorcerer who could only be killed by a god?

"Rakshovidhva Nsakarakaya discovered where Krong Reap has hidden the Maitreya. We have collected an army of adepts from the Shaolin Monastery. They await us at the pass near his hideout."

The abbot ushered them back into the great hall. Anne grabbed Michael's arm as they walked. "The pass? That sounds downright frigid."

"Yes, but do you realize who Rakshovidhva Nsakarakaya is?"

Before he could tell her, Yeshe shushed them. She stood before the dais where the abbot usually sat and spread her arms wide, chanting as she had in their hotel room miles away. A flicker of light quickly grew into a golden portal in the middle of the hall. The monks took it all in stride and continued their chants uninterrupted.

This time Yeshe stepped through first. The abbot gestured for them to follow. Cold wind slammed into Anne and she stumbled back into Michael just as he walked through. Tahir appeared next. He grimaced as the wind pelted them with tiny shards of ice. Rainey looked like she was on a beach in Mexico.

The nuns she visited must have taught her some secrets, but before Anne could ask about it, Yeshe stalked ahead.

They followed a narrow path that clung to the rocky mountain side. Anne tried not to stare at the precipitous drop on her left. She caught a glint of silver way below. A river?

"Best not to look down," Rainey said from behind her. "The body follows the eyes."

Anne jerked her head forward. "Right. Do you know where we are?"

"Not really," Rainey answered. "We're still in the Himalayas."

"That much is clear," Anne said. Her teeth felt like they would freeze and snap off, so she closed her mouth.

The group rounded a corner and the rock opened out into a wider recess in the mountainside. A collection of monks stood waiting, their gray and sandstone colored robes blending with the rocks. As one, they put their palms together and bowed to Yeshe and Abbot Choki. These must be the Shaolin monks. A man who appeared to be their leader stepped forward and the three spoke, maybe in Chinese. Anne couldn't be sure.

After a minute, Yeshe nodded and turned to the crystal holders. "They have cleared the way up to the temple steps. Do not be alarmed by what you see on the way."

'Don't be alarmed.' Right. Just like 'don't picture an elephant,' Anne thought. Works every time.

The monks led the way single file. After a few more switchbacks, the path widened out and a temple appeared on the rise in front of them. An enormous craggy peak thrust up into the sky behind it, dwarfing the structure. The three tiers ended in thin points making the temple look like a flock of birds trying to launch themselves into the thin air. Ordinarily, Anne would appreciate its beauty.

What looked like gray and tan rocks lay scattered ahead,

but as they came closer, she realized the rocks were actually bodies sprawled on the ground, the snow around some stained poppy red. One lay with a spear still piercing his heart. Another's head was twisted at a sickening angle. The fallen wore sand camouflage which blended with the snow and rocks. Anne wondered where these uniforms had come from. None of the dead wore the robes of the Shaolin. She moved a little closer to Michael.

The builders had flatted out a small plaza in front of the temple steps where a dozen or so men knelt knee-deep in snow around the perimeter, heads bowed and hands tied behind their backs. Piles of automatic rifles and various knives lay far to the side. Four monks guarded them. One looked up and caught Anne's eye, a malicious sneer on his face.

Were four Shaolin enough to contain all these men, Anne wondered. She glanced at Rainey, the question in her eyes. She seemed to understand the doubt and gave a clipped nod of reassurance. Rainey went back to scanning for threats, letting her eyes roam over the assembled men and the terrain around them. She and Arnold kept the crystal key holders in a close circle.

Yeshe and Abbot Choki paused in front of the steps to the small temple. They looked at each other, then faced forward and closed their eyes. Anne felt a tug on her inner vision, but she didn't close her eyes. Not with all these enemy soldiers around. After about a minute, the two opened their eyes again and started up the steps without a word or a glance back. The group scrambled to follow.

They stepped up to a brick porch that ran completely around the square shrine. A white fence on the edge protected visitors from plunging into the chasm below. Two vultures sat on the tier above calmly cleaning their feathers.

"That's not too ominous," Anne whispered to Michael.

"This may be a sky temple," Rainey said, matching Anne's tone.

"That fits. We're on the edge of this cliff," Anne said.

"A sky temple is a burial site."

Anne looked around. "I don't see any graves."

Michael's chuckle was humorless. "A sky temple is where traditional Tibetan Buddhists leave the bodies of the deceased out for decomposition. The carrion birds help things along."

Anne grimaced. "This just keeps getting better."

Abbot Choki approached the red and gold double doors set in the western entrance. He put his ear to the surface, then indicated they should wait while he and Yeshe entered. They left the door open, so Anne moved closer to peer inside. Everyone followed her. The interior looked similar to any Tibetan structure. Brightly colored pillars lined each side of a central walkway. She couldn't make out the statue at the end. Yeshe appeared again and waved them inside.

The group turned left and headed to the wall where steps led to the second tier. Behind them, Anne heard soft swishing. She turned to see soldiers pouring out from between the southern pillars. Fifty, a hundred, then more. Too many. Some wore the sand camouflage uniforms she'd seen on the bodies outside, but others wore all black. Masks covered their mouth and nose. Fierce eyes glared as they advanced with the deadly grace of panthers.

Ninjas, Anne thought. That was the only word to describe them.

The Shaolin closed on them. With a shout, the ninjas drew their weapons. Curved swords, short daggers. Some carried nun chucks. This did not stop the monks. They did not draw any weapons, but took crouched in fighting stances in front of the crystal holders and beckoned them forward.

Arnold had no such compunction. He pulled a revolver

Anne hadn't known he was carrying, dropped to one knee and took aim. One man fell, then a second. Rainey ran to the other side of the monks and turned into a flurry of fists and feet.

A man in black broke through the line and ran toward Tahir, who put up his fists. But he was older now and not trained in martial arts. He didn't stand a chance. The man batted Tahir's punches away and twisted his arm behind him, ratcheting it up high. Tahir rose on his toes to avoid the pain. The ninja grabbed the chain holding Tahir's crystal from around his neck and broke it with a jerk.

The sorcerer's army had one key. A shudder ran through the temple. The atmosphere darkened.

Anne reacted without thought. She sprinted toward the man in black and kicked his knee from the side. He stumbled, but recovered quickly and turned to her. A fist flew toward her face, but she'd already ducked. She came up under the man's arm and delivered a blow to his kidney.

He just turned his head and smiled at her. But then his eyes glazed and he fell. Half his head was blown away.

Anne blinked. She'd been so focused she hadn't heard the shot.

Arnold gave her a crisp nod and turned back to the soldiers, taking aim again.

Yeshe moved up the steps, urging the crystal holders to follow, but Anne lingered, still watching. Michael grabbed her arm. "Let's go."

She shook him off. Her blood was up. "You want to get trapped up there? With this army at our backs?"

They looked at the sea of fighters. More and more soldiers lay dead on the temple floor, some with gunshot wounds, others with no visible sign of injury. At that moment, Arnold threw his pistol away and waded into the soldiers.

"No more bullets," Michael whispered.

Arnold seemed to spot Rainey on the opposite side of the crowd. "Meet you in the middle?" he shouted.

"I'll be first."

"It's a bet."

Anne shook her head. They almost seemed to be enjoying themselves.

A few Shaolin monks moved in a wedge into the black robed fighters, driving them into the fists of a ring of monks on either side. The ninjas were now surrounded. Within minutes, they lay dead in the middle of the temple floor. The few remaining soldiers turned and ran.

A few of the Shaolin remained to check the bodies to be sure none would rise to fight again. Like the demon had, Anne thought with a shiver. The crystal holders joined Yeshe and Abbot Choki at the foot of the stairs and started up. As they climbed, between the lattice that formed the wall Anne caught a glimpse of the statue at the end of the hall. A black female figure sat, her mouth open, a red tongue protruding between sharp, white fangs, her eyes wide with rage. Around her neck hung a garland of severed heads.

Kali. The Dark Mother. Goddess of Time and Destruction. This temple was dedicated to Kali.

Before Anne could call Michael's attention to the statue, they stepped out on the next tier, a simpler hall with a wooden floor. Half the monks and Arnold continued up the final flight of stairs.

Anne supposed it made some sense that a burial site would have a Kali statue. When Dr. Abernathy had first started training her, he'd insisted she read several world mythologies. If she remembered correctly, Kali was considered a compassionate goddess. An embodiment of the Divine Mother. Anne took some solace from this.

"Take these dead into your heart, Mother," Anne whispered.

As they climbed the next flight of stairs, low mutterings reached her ears. They grew closer. A rhythmic chant and the name Kali Ma was repeated frequently among the otherwise unrecognizable Sanskrit. The chant was off kilter. Somehow discordant, menacing.

Anne slowed, dizzy. Her stomach threatened to turn over. Then the words began to make sense to her.

"Holy Kali, Ancient Terror, I offer this sacrifice to you."

"Is he speaking English?" Michael asked.

"No, Arabic," Tahir said.

"With this ceremony, grant me your power, O Dreadful One."

Some magic was translating the words.

The group of crystal holders stopped in their tracks. Bile rose in Anne's throat. But Rainey pushed up behind her. "Take heart. We are with Yeshe. You have your crystal."

Anne fished the pendant holding the crystal key out from beneath her blouse and held it in the palm of her hand. Warmth pulsed through the stone that synched up with her own heartbeat. Yes, she was a crystal holder. She was not alone. She had fought a black robed ninja. She could face whatever lay ahead.

The group emerged onto an open pavilion topped with a sloping roof. The wind whipped through Anne's thin clothes. Her eyes watered, blurring her vision. She got behind Michael to hide from the gust.

He stopped abruptly and she ran into him. "Oh, my God."

"What?" Anne stepped up beside him.

A tall figure moved, arms raised, swaying and chanting, dressed in layers of diaphanous black material that floated in the wind. He circled a statue swathed in white robes that lay recumbent on a platform in the middle of the room.

Yeshe and the abbot moved closer, the three crystal holders close behind. Anne noticed the cloth across the statue's chest rise. "It's so windy," she whispered.

"That's not the wind," Tahir murmured.

The cloth fell, then rose again. The statue was breathing. They were staring at a living man.

Not just any man, Anne realized. They'd found the Maitreya Buddha.

But he was unconscious.

Anne lifted her eyes from the inert figure to find the sorcerer staring at her. He looked exactly like one of the asura heads in the Angkor National Museum, complete with bulging eyes and a wide nose that dominated his face. He radiated a power that might block out the sun. When her eyes met his, the frown changed to a terrifying grin, white fangs gleaming. "Neang Seda. You have come at last."

Oh no, this couldn't be good. He thought she was Neang Seda, the wife of Preah Ream. Sita to Lord Ram.

The sorcerer took a step toward her. The thick menace pouring off him grew stronger. Four Shaolin monks moved to block his path, but he ignored them. "You are as beautiful as the stories tell. Come, join your lord." He gestured to the platform where the Maitreya Buddha lay unconscious. "Together, you will make a most glorious sacrifice."

Terror stole over Anne's limbs. Her body grew heavy and rigid, her breath shallow.

"You seem to have your stories mixed up, Krong Reap." Abbot Choki's voice was a crack of light in the dark storm clouds of the sorcerer's energy.

Krong Reap's gaze shifted to the abbot and Anne could breathe again. Barely.

"Wasn't it your son who tried to sacrifice Preah Ream to Kali? He hoped to gain the deva's powers."

The sorcerer grinned, his fangs catching his lip. Blood welled up. "I am not hidebound to tradition as you are, monk. Mahiravana had the right idea. We will harness the power of Kali and stop the pollution of his light from rising." He pointed to the Maitreya Buddha.

As Abbot Choki and Krong Reap talked, Yeshe quietly gathered the crystal holders. "You go to the west," she whispered in Anne's ear. She took Michael's arm and guided him to the north. Tahir pointed to the southern side of the temple and Yeshe nodded. She took her place in the east. The Shaolin moved with them, distributing themselves on the perimeter of their tight circle.

As the others took their places, Anne's gaze fell on the face of the man lying on the platform. Peace radiated from him, even under the spell of the sorcerer. The center of her chest warmed and a wave of light spread down deep into the earth below and up past her crown, past the point an arm's length above, into the sun that she knew still shone above the clouds. Power flowed.

Anne's thoughts and fears dropped away. She soared into that glorious state she'd experienced in Egypt and again beneath the Tor in Glastonbury. When giving birth to Arthur. When standing beneath the tunnels in Peru inside the city of light. All her limitations fell away and her heart burst with joy.

Michael smiled at her from his place in the circle and she knew he felt it too. That his mind had merged with the great universal consciousness. Tahir's head fell back as he reveled in the light.

Yeshe nodded, satisfied. They each took their crystal key into their hand, the base resting in the palms, the point aligned with their index fingers. They pointed the clear stones at the

Buddha resting on the platform. With a breath, Anne channeled the column of light through the key and into the man who had come to enlighten the world.

"No!" Krong Reap screamed. "You can't have him." He tossed the abbot across the room. Anne heard the snap of a bone breaking. Tears ran down her cheeks, but she couldn't break off from the circle to help the abbot.

The Buddha stirred. Anne felt him climbing back to consciousness. His head turned and he opened his eyes.

"No!" Too fast even for the Shaolin monks, Krong rushed to Tahir and grabbed his arm pointing the crystal, pushing it up, breaking the circuit.

Anne cried out as the tidal wave of energy rebound against her, knocking her to the floor. The Buddha's eyes closed. He sunk back into unconsciousness.

Krong ran toward Yeshe. The monks on either side of her moved to intercept him, but he swept them away a wave of magic. He grabbed the Tibetan nun by the throat and held her up off the floor. "You will not win this time." He spat the words in her face.

Yeshe struggled in the demon's grip, her legs kicking as if she were dangling from a noose. Michael darted toward him, but Krong knocked him back with another wave of malevolent energy. The sorcerer carried Yeshe to the platform and muttered a phrase. More Shaolin monks ran toward him and bounced off an invisible shield. Krong laid Yeshe next to the Maitreya Buddha. Passing a hand over her face and muttering another magical phrase, her eyes closed.

Anne lay on the stone floor, weeping. This could not be the end of all their work. They'd opened the galactic portal in Egypt. Saved White Spring in Glastonbury and closed the time loop to Atlantis. They'd defeated Mordred and she'd given birth to Arthur, the once and future king. And finally, they'd brought forth this great Buddha in Peru. An enlightened one meant to bring the sacred teachings to earth in this time. Now, he lay unconscious with Yeshe insensible beside him. Abbot Choki's dead body sprawled on the floor nearby

Anne glanced at the abbot, thinking to send a prayer for his soul at least. She gasped when she saw his spirit standing tall above his body like the flame of a Christmas candle, unwavering. He smiled beatifically. Did he know something that she didn't or was it simply the wider vision of the other world that made him smile?

Beside him another candle flame flickered to life, only there was no beeswax taper like the ones Grandmother Elizabeth always lit for Christmas dinner. This flame hung in the air. Another portal was forming. It widened, brightened until Anne threw a hand up to shield her eyes. Light flowed out. And hope.

Krong Reap turned toward the brilliant disc of light, a frown darkening his face.

The flow of energy through Anne's body returned. She stood, groping for her crystal. From behind the spirit of Abbot Choki another form began to take shape. The light gelled into a material body that towered above the abbot. The bare arms and chest rippled with muscle. Powerful, naked thighs stepped forward. A sash of red silk bordered in gold swathed his hips. Gold arm and wrist bands matched a gold torque around his neck. On his head sat a golden crown and in one hand rested a giant gada, a golden club. Something floated behind the figure. It looked like a tail. But that wasn't possible. This was a human —then Anne's eyes moved to his face and found a monkey looking back at her.

"What?" she said in a small voice.

"Lord Hanuman," Michael said. "Remember Yeshe said Rakshovidhva Nsakarakaya had discovered where the Maitreya Buddha was hidden?"

Before Anne could respond, the sorcerer roared only to be answered by the louder growl of the Monkey King. They stalked toward each other, Hanuman swinging his gada. Krong made a gesture and two gold shields appeared, one in each hand. He raised them, meeting the club with a thunderous clang. Hanuman swung again, this time shattering one of the shields.

"Ravana," he shouted. "You think to fool me coming as Krong Reap? How have you returned?"

"Some kind man found my prison and set me free."

Hanuman shook his head. "My Lord Rama dispensed with you ages ago."

"He did not succeed," the demon laughed, the sound freezing Anne's blood, driving hope away.

Hanuman waved his hand and some measure of warmth returned.

The two massive beings continued to circle each other looking for a weakness. With Krong's attention focused on his ancient enemy, his spell began to unravel. Yeshe's eyes opened. Groggy at first, she managed to sit up. Her eyes flew wide when she saw Lord Hanuman. She put her fingers to the pulse on the Maitreya's neck and nodded her head. He was still alive.

Yeshe slid off the platform and snapped her fingers, getting the attention of the crystal holders. She pointed to the directions, and Anne, Michael, and Tahir scrambled to take up their positions. The remaining Shaolin monks took up their positions.

Anne placed her crystal in her palm and aimed it at the Buddha, praying for the flood of energy to return. Yeshe began a soft chant that coiled below the shouts and blows of the two warring deities. Anne added her voice. Michael's baritone sounded and Tahir joined in. Something stirred inside her. Her chest warmed. Light flowed from above, joining the earth's stream from below.

"Stop them," shouted the sorcerer, but there was no one to help him.

The streams of energy met in her heart and ignited, blazing like a meteor as it roared through her. Anne's crystal lit up along with the other three and light bright as a laser shot out into the Maitreya.

His eyes flew open. He sat up, taking in his surroundings. He smiled when he saw the Monkey King. "Hanuman, my defender."

The sorcerer's shields melted away.

"My Lord," the Monkey King shouted and brought his gada down on Krong Reap's head.

The sorcerer let out a horrific scream, then fell. His body twitched on the floor in a gruesome display, then finally stopped. The oppressive darkness lifted completely and full consciousness flooded through Anne. Through the link in the crystal keys, she felt Michael and Tahir's joy as they merged with the One Consciousness. Anne felt a click, like a seat belt closing, and she knew that this time she would not lose her connection to the higher realm again.

Hanuman smiled at them. He lifted his hands, palms toward them. "The crystal holders have fulfilled their mission. You have earned this gift of enlightenment. Return home and watch as the Awakening spreads through the earth."

The Maitreya Buddha came to each of them, blessing them, murmuring his thanks. Yeshe watched from her place in the east, radiant. Then the Buddha went to Arnold and Rainey. With a wave of his hand, blood washed away as their wounds closed. Bruises faded beneath his hands. Their faces lit with bliss. He blessed each of the Shaolin.

As he did, Yeshe gestured for the crystal holders and Arnold to move to one side of the pavilion. "Ready?"

Anne looked at Michael. "It seems so sudden, but yes."

Arnold glanced at Rainey. Yeshe patted his shoulder. "She will join you later."

The Tibetan nun took a wide stance and repeated the gestures and phrases she'd used before. A small light glowed and quickly spread to a round, shimmering light, just like the surface of a swimming pool. Yeshe bowed, palms together. "I thank you for your service, shining ones."

Anne smiled. "Come visit. Arthur would love to see you."

Yeshe nodded, but somehow Anne knew this was the last time she would ever see her. On impulse, she hugged her.

Yeshe laughed. "Do not disturb my concentration. Now off with you now." She gestured to the portal.

Arnold stepped through first, followed by Tahir. Michael took Anne's hand and gave it a squeeze. "Ready?"

Try as she might, Anne took a deep breath and held it as she stepped through. With the next step, Strains of "O Holy Night" rang out. They'd emerged in a secluded corner of their Cambodian hotel, the same one they'd found Yeshe, Tahir, and Rainey in when this adventure had begun. It seemed like days.

They walked out to see a Cambodian family smiling at the camera, having their picture taken in front of the giant Christmas tree. Anne reached her hand into her pocket and found her cell phone. She pressed a button and it switched on. They'd been gone six hours.

"It's a Christmas miracle," she declared. "Come on. Let's take our picture." She asked the Cambodian family if someone would snap a shot of them in front of the tree. They bowed their acceptance. She, Michael, Tahir, and Arnold lined up in front of the towering tree and smiled.

The husband took the picture.

"You shine like star," the wife said to them.

The man handed the phone back to Anne. "Is good?"

"It's perfect," Anne said. "Everything is perfect."

They all bowed and the couple headed for the door of the hotel.

She turned to the group. "Tahir, want to spend Christmas with us?"

"It would be a fitting end to our adventure," he said, his face glowing.

About the Author

Theresa Crater brings ancient temples, lost civilizations, and secret societies back to life in her visionary fiction. She is the author of the Power Places and Mystic Assassin series as well as stand-alone novels. Her short stories explore ancient myth brought into the present day.

For more information:

www.theresalcrater.com
theresa@theresalcrater.com

Want to Join My Newsletter?

Signup for news and special offers!
https://landing.mailerlite.com/webforms/landing/z5m5w8

Also By

Theresa Crater

Power Places Series

A forgotten family legacy. Six crystal keys. One shot at unlocking the secrets beneath the Sphinx. Buy *Under the Stone Paw*

Beneath the Hallowed Hill

Two legendary worlds. A disaster in the making. Can her psychic powers avert catastrophe? Buy *Beneath the Hallowed Hill*

Return of the Grail King

The long-awaited King Arthur returns to be reborn in the 21st century, but an old enemy from the past rises to stop him. Buy *Return of the Grail King*

Into the City of Light

These legendary mystics want a peaceful life. But with the fate of humanity hanging in the balance, a new mission brings them too close to darkness. Buy *Into the City of Light*

Power Places Box Set: Books 1-3

Includes *Under the Stone Paw, Beneath the Hallowed Hill,* and *Return of the Grail King.* Buy *Power Places Box Set, Books 1-3*

Yuletide Tales

A collection of winter holiday short stories featuring the Power Places cast of characters. Buy Yuletide Tales.

Power Places Short Stories

"Frankincense and Myrrh"

Anne isn't letting Michael relax on Christmas Day. She's sent him on a treasure hunt inside the big Le Clair family house. Buy "Frankincense and Myrrh"

"Festival of Lights"

When Michael takes Anne and Arthur to celebrate the first night of Chanukah with his family, they're all in for a big surprise. Buy "Festival of Lights"

"A Star, A Star"

Morning Star, O cheering sight! 'Ere thou cam'st, how dark earth's night! A brilliant, new star appears at Christmas in 2020. What does it foretell? Buy "A Star, A Star"

"Summer Solstice"

That child! Where did he disappear to now? Anne Le Clair talks Grandmother Elizabeth into celebrating summer solstice in Glastonbury. Little Arthur decides to pay a visit to another king. Will they find him before he gets lost in time? **Buy "Summer Solstice"**

"Cup o'Kindness"

On New Year's Eve, Grandmother Elizabeth invites the group to unpack their adventures in Peru. They feel their work is finished . . . until the Tibetan mystic Yeshe pops in to tell them she needs their help. Buy "Cup o'Kindness"

"A Merry Buddhist Christmas"

When you're heading home for Christmas, but that pesky Tibetan nun says you have to save the world one more time. Buy "A Merry Buddhist Christmas"

Related Novel

The Star Family

Whoever holds the key decides the future of humanity. when mysterious nighttime chanting leads Jane Frey to a secret chamber, she becomes entangled in a clandestine society with unsettling aims. Buy *The Star Family*

SPIRIT SPRINGS

Spirit Springs Short Stories

"The Veils Thin"

It's Samhain. The veils thin and the spirits walk. Kyleigh Matthews hopes to get a glimpse of her wife who recently passed away. She despairs when the portal starts to close, but who should appear but the Morrigan accompanied by none other than Blair, her beloved – with a message for the whole town. Buy "The Veils Thin"

SHORT STORIES

"The Judgment of Osiris"

On the last day of the tour he leads, Owen accepts a gift from a rival tour guide Simon that contains a deadly poison. Will resurrection come for him as it did for his namesake Osiris or will his soul be consumed by Ammit? Buy "The Judgment of Osiris"

"Bringing the Waters"

Nebit and Khai celebrate the Sacred Marriage. Each year the High Priestess of Hathor and High Priest of Horus unite sexually to bring on the flooding of the Nile. But this year, Nebit has another mission. Buy "Bringing the Waters"

"White Moon"

When we call the Ancient Ones, sometimes they come. When Mayan Goddess Ixchel comes for her divine lover, lost in human form, her presence challenges the couples around her. Buy "White Moon"

OTHER BOOKS FROM CRYSTAL STAR PUBLISHING

T.L. Crater

MYSTIC ASSASSIN SERIES

Assassin Awakens

She's got a to-do list to die for. But can this contract killer take down the most powerful man in the world? Buy *Assassin Awakens*

Breached: A Mystic Assassin Novella

Washington compromised. Insurrection rising. There's only one woman for the job... Buy *Breached*

Louise Ryder

School of Hard Knocks

Three generations of women. A devastating connection. Can they endure their personal tragedies? Buy *School of Hard Knocks*

God in a Box

It's the guru invasion of the 1980s. After spending her life savings to fly to Europe and become a meditation teacher, Stacey is told to go home. Lesbians are not welcome. She's lost the love of her life already. Will she lose the other half of her dreams now? Buy *God in a Box*

SHORT STORIES

"Solstice"

Certain she's left something important in her childhood home, Elizabeth visits, only to discover what she's lost is not an object, but a memory. Buy "Solstice"

"Still Shots"

She danced like she was the only woman on the floor. She closed her eyes and moved stomach, hips and round sleek thighs. I promised not to fall in love. But you know how that goes. Buy "Still Shots"

www.ingramcontent.com/pod-product-compliance
Lightning Source LLC
Chambersburg PA
CBHW022049170626
46808CB00003B/1411